P9-DWS-792

CALGARY PUBLIC LIBRARY

NOV   2019

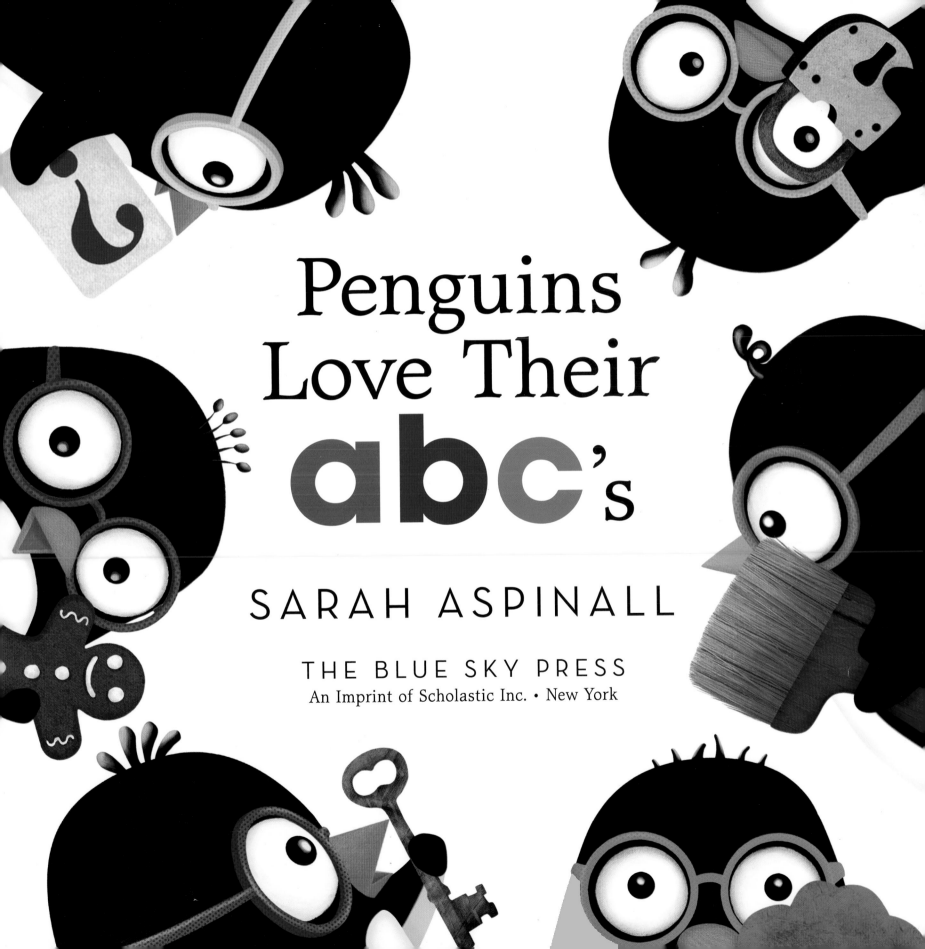

Penguins Love Their abc's

SARAH ASPINALL

THE BLUE SKY PRESS

An Imprint of Scholastic Inc. • New York

For Mum and Dad—
Your sustained commitment to collecting
hundreds and hundreds of chocolate eggs,
and then hiding them in the garden for us
to seek each year, was rather extraordinary.
Thank you for two-and-a-half decades
worth of feverish excitement. xo

THE BLUE SKY PRESS

Copyright © 2017 by Sarah Aspinall

All rights reserved. Published by The Blue Sky Press,
an imprint of Scholastic Inc., *Publishers since 1920.*
SCHOLASTIC, THE BLUE SKY PRESS, and associated logos
are trademarks and/or registered trademarks of Scholastic Inc.

The publisher does not have any control over and does not assume any
responsibility for author or third-party websites or their content. No
part of this publication may be reproduced, stored in a retrieval system,
or transmitted in any form or by any means, electronic, mechanical,
photocopying, recording, or otherwise, without written permission of the
publisher. For information regarding permission, please write to: Permissions
Department, Scholastic Inc., 557 Broadway, New York, New York 10012.

This book is a work of fiction. Names, characters, places, and incidents
are either the product of the author's imagination or are used fictitiously,
and any resemblance to actual persons, living or dead, business
establishments, events, or locales is entirely coincidental.

Library of Congress catalog card number available

ISBN 978-1-338-13420-9

10 9 8 7 6 5 4 3 2 1   17 18 19 20 21

Printed in China   38
First edition, September 2017

Book design by Sarah Aspinall and Kathleen Westray

Once there were six little penguins—
six little penguins who loved to play
games with the alphabet.

Today they had put on their special
hide-and-seek glasses because . . .

. . . the penguins were going on an Alphabet Hunt!

Tulip, Tiger Lily, Dandelion, Bluebell, Violet, and Broccoli were ready to start looking for letters.

But did the little penguins even
know all the letters of the alphabet?

Do *you* know?

They needed to find:
a b c d e f g h i j k l m
n o p q r s t u v w x y z.

"Here's an apple!" said
Tulip with surprise.
"A is for apple!"

Mama Penguin had hidden all the letters in the snow, and above each letter, she had placed a clue.

Do you think these six little penguins can guess what letter is under each clue?

Can *you*?

"The letter b!"
said Broccoli.
"Like my name!"

Do you know the
first letter of *your* name?

a is for apple . . . b is for broccoli . . .

c is for cactus . . . d is for duck . . .

e *is*

for

egg . . .

f is for flowers . . .

"I like flowers,"
said Dandelion.
"Especially yellow ones."

Which color flower do *you* like best?

"Look! A heart!" said Tulip.
"Let's give it to someone we love!" said Violet.
"I know who we can give it to,"
said Bluebell.

i is for ice cream . . .

k is for key . . .

l is for lock . . .

But what
comes next?
Do *you* know?

Broccoli does!

"Oooh! Everything is bigger!" He giggled.

m is for magnifying glass . . .

n is for noodles... **o** is for orange...

"I can balance it on my head!" said Tiger Lily.

p is for paintbrush . . .

q is for question mark . . .

r is for radish . . .

"Wheeeeeeee!" yelled Violet as she rolled down the hill.

S is for skis . . .

t is for tire . . .

u is for underpants!

"Yippee! Yahoo!
Whoopee!" shouted all
of the penguins together.
"Our lucky underpants!
Just what we need to help
us find the rest of the letters!"

V is for vase . . .

W is for wheelbarrow . . .

X is for X-ray . . .

Y is for yo-yo . . .

Z is for zucchini!

"We did it!" said the penguins.
"We found the whole alphabet!"

But how would they carry
all the letters back to Mama?

In the wheelbarrow, of course!

"Hooray!"
cheered Mama.
"What clever
little penguins
you are! Now
can you put the
letters in the right
order?" she asked.

Yes, they could! And
they said the alphabet
out loud—in order, too!

abcdefghijklmn

Mama was so pleased.

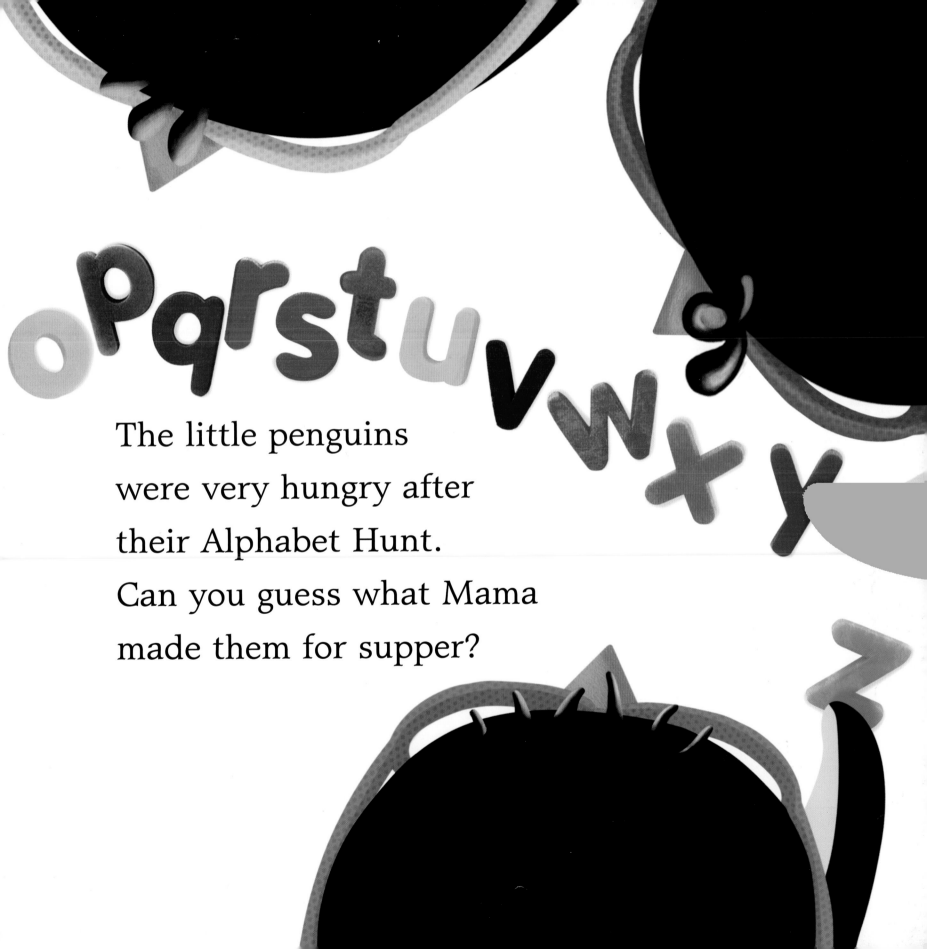

The little penguins were very hungry after their Alphabet Hunt. Can you guess what Mama made them for supper?

Alphabet soup!

Yummy, yummy, yummy!

They gobbled down every drop.

"We love our abc's, and we love alphabet soup," said the little penguins. "But not as much as we love . . .

AaBbCcDdEeFfGgHhIiJjKkLlMmNn